DISCARDED BY
ONTARIO CITY LIBRARY

14.95

D0606815

ONTARIO CITY LIBRARY

APR   1991

ONTARIO, CA 91764

WHEN AFRICA
WAS HOME

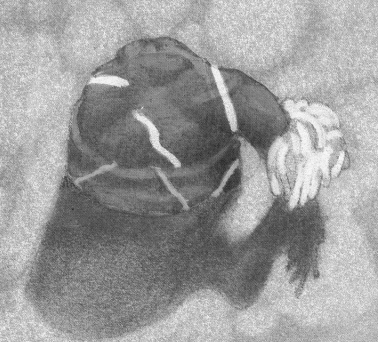

by Karen Lynn Williams
pictures by Floyd Cooper

Orchard Books · New York

Text copyright © 1991 by Karen Lynn Williams
Illustrations copyright © 1991 by Floyd Cooper
All rights reserved. No part of this book may be reproduced or transmitted in any form or by any means, electronic or mechanical, including photocopying, recording or by any information storage or retrieval system, without permission in writing from the Publisher.

Orchard Books, A division of Franklin Watts, Inc.
387 Park Avenue South, New York, NY 10016

Manufactured in the United States of America. Printed by General Offset Company, Inc.
Bound by Horowitz/Rae. Book design by Mina Greenstein.
The text of this book is set in 15 pt. Kennerly.
The illustrations are oil wash on board, reproduced in full color.
10 9 8 7 6 5 4 3 2 1

Library of Congress Cataloging-in-Publication Data
Williams, Karen Lynn. When Africa was home / by Karen Lynn Williams ; paintings by
Floyd Cooper.   p. cm.
Summary: After returning to the United States, Peter's whole family misses the warmth and friendliness
of their life in Africa; so Peter's father looks for another job there. "A Richard Jackson book."
ISBN 0-531-05925-1.   ISBN 0-531-08525-2 (lib.)
[1. Africa—Fiction.] I. Cooper, Floyd, ill. II. Title. PZ7.W66655Wh 1991 E—dc20
90-7684 CIP AC

For Peter so that he will always remember when
Africa was home.
And in memory of his grandfather, George C. Williams,
whose support helped make it all come true.
 K. L. W.

To Dayton Michael, for coming home.
 F. C.

When Peter was small, he rode on his nanny's back, tied snugly in a bright cloth. The rocking of her strong body soothed him. Peter called his nanny "*Mayi*," the word which means mother in the Chichewa language. When Africa was home, Peter had two mothers.

"*Achimwene*," Yekha and the other children called him. Little brother.

When Peter grew older, he and his friends slid down anthills and shimmied up paw-paw trees. They chased the cows from the maize fields and made toys from the smooth white stalks. They made dolls with wet earth from the riverbed.

"Such a child with golden hair should not play in the sun," Peter's mayi warned.

"Wear a hat," his mother said.

When Africa was home, Peter played from the time the sun was still cool until his shadow danced in the moonlight—and he never wore a hat.

"The son of your father must wear shoes," his mayi scolded.
"You'll hurt your feet," his mother agreed.

But when Africa was home, Peter knew better. He ran
races with his friends. His feet were hard and never felt
the pebbles. The warm earth felt good. *How could he climb
a mango tree with shoes on?*

"In America everyone wears shoes," Peter's mother
explained.

"Not me," said Peter.

"You must get used to wearing shoes," his mother said.
"Soon we'll be in America—we'll all be going home when
Daddy's work here is done."

That's not my home, Peter thought.

In the African sun, Peter's legs grew long and his skin tan.
"You've grown so dark," his father said one day.

Peter held his arm next to Yekha's, and he knew he wasn't that dark. They stuck their tongues out at each other and laughed. That's the way it was when Africa was home.

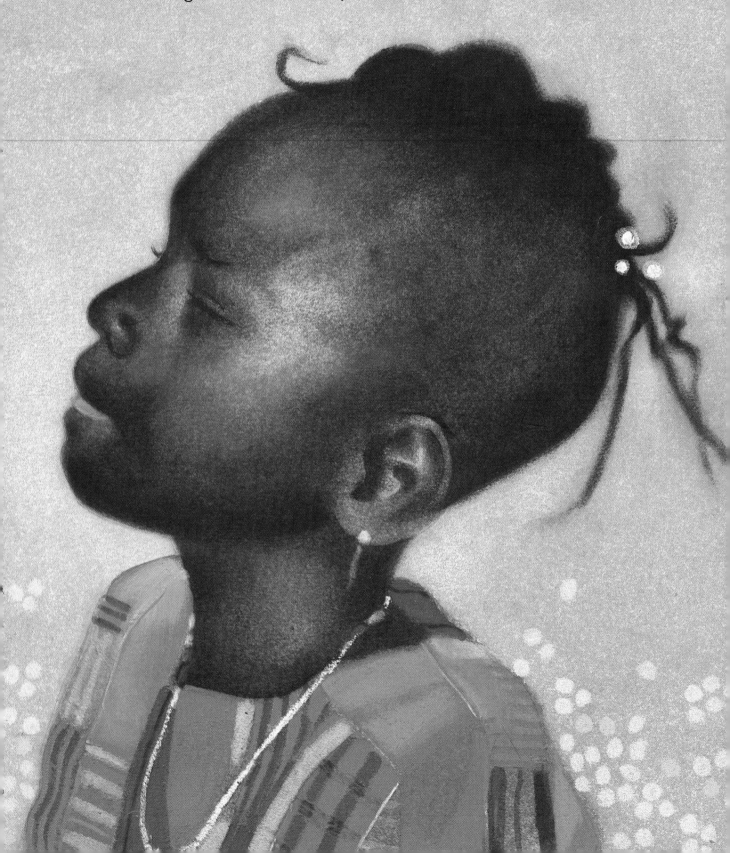

In Africa, Peter ran with the goats and chased the chickens. He screeched back at the monkeys and frightened a whole herd of antelope with one clap of his hands.

"Maybe we'll get a kitten in America," Peter's father told him the day they began to pack.

"I don't want a kitten," Peter said. "I don't want to go to America."

At dinner that night, Peter said, "I'm not hungry," and ran to the home of his mayi.

Seated on the ground, Peter and Yekha shared a meal from the same bowl, as they often did. Peter rolled the warm corn paste in his hand to make a ball. Then he dipped it into the sauce. Sometimes it was fish sauce and he ate the eyes and all. Even fish eyes tasted good when Africa was home.

"In America it's polite to eat with a fork and a spoon," Peter's mother told him later.

"I won't," Peter said crossly. "I'm not going."

"My work here is finished," his father explained. "Someday, perhaps we'll come back if I find another job in Africa. But soon we must go home to America."

"This is my home here." Peter stamped his foot. His father frowned. They could hear happy voices outside.

"Your friends are calling you," his mother said. "Go play awhile before bed."

From his bed that night Peter looked out at the big African sky. The stars were so bright it seemed he could almost reach out and touch them. He could hear the hippos moo and the hyenas groan and the drums sing in the distance.

With a mosquito net tucked all around him, Peter felt comfortable and safe. *How would he sleep without one in America?*

In the morning Mayi asked, as she always did, "How
have you slept?"

And Peter asked Yekha, "How have you slept?"

"I have slept well," she and Mayi answered, as they
did every day.

"I have slept well," Peter said too.

That afternoon it was hot. Mayi gave Peter and Yekha
a coin. At the corner by the big road, they bought a
stick of sugarcane. In the purple shade of the jacaranda
they chewed the stiff, stringy pieces of cane and sweet
juice ran down their chins.

When Africa was home, even the sticks tasted delicious.

"In America," Mother promised, "we'll eat Popsicles
that are as cold as ice."

Peter did not know what ice was.

When Africa was home, he and his mayi chatted in a
language that was fast and musical: the words sounded
like their ideas.

How will I know all the words I need in America? Peter
wondered.

To his mayi he said, "It is far to America."

"Indeed," she agreed.

When the time came to say good-bye, Mayi said to him:
"Go well, little son."

"Go well," Yekha echoed.

"Stay well," Peter told them both sadly.

His parents' white car bumped over the dusty dirt road.
Peter whispered, "*Ndizabweronso*" to the passing
cornfields and the dark brown earth. I will come back.

Peter and his family drove through fifty-seven dips and around and around and up and up the mountain. Up and out of the steamy village they drove into the cool air. Into a city that was big and noisy.

They boarded an airplane that was bigger than a house.
There were hundreds of seats and tiny windows and
buttons and dials and switches.
The airplane flew through the day and a night.
And then Peter was in America.
People talk funny, he thought.
No one stopped to say "Hello" and ask how he had slept.

Winter came in America and icy cold snow fell on the ground. Peter missed the warm rains of Africa. In his new snowsuit and heavy boots, he felt like a statue.

His mother made him a bright red ski cap. The yellow and blue designs reminded Peter of home in Africa. He wore the hat all the time, even indoors, and waited for the time when Africa would be his home again.

"Is it time to go back yet?" Peter asked each day.

"Not yet," his father always answered.

In America, Peter watched a box with people inside who talked. His mother used a long snake to clean the floor. It ate his toys.

"I want to go home," Peter said.

In America Peter ate pizza with his fingers, but he never sat on the floor when he ate. Peter missed Mayi's warm corn paste.

The big city lights made nighttime a dull gray, and the stars seemed far away. In America, Peter missed Yekha and Mayi.

Peter, his father and mother all missed Africa.

Peter waited. One day his father said, "I've found another job. Now it's time. We can go back."

"Back to Africa," his mother said.

"Home," said Peter and he happily took off his heavy snowsuit and clumsy boots, but he kept on his bright red ski cap.

On the airplane, Peter traveled back through the night and a day. But still he was not home. In the car he went down and around the mountain and through the fifty-seven dips. Toward the village.

"Going home takes a long time," Peter said.

His father laughed. "It's not far now."

And when their car came down the valley, Yekha ran
with the other children to greet it.

"*Peter akubwera.*" Peter is coming. "Peter, Peter," the
children shouted, running alongside the car.

Yekha brought him a mango. Mayi brought a chicken.

"You are fat," they said—for in Africa it is polite to
say so.

Peter pulled off his shoes and wriggled his toes in the
dusty dirt.

"Your feet are soft," his friends teased.

Peter took off his bright red, yellow, and blue ski cap
and gave it to Yekha. Everyone tried it on.

"*Zikomo,*" Yekha said. Thank you. "You have come,"
she said, smiling.

"*Kwatu*," Peter said. Home. And Peter in his bare feet
and Yekha in her red ski cap raced to the top of an anthill.